Leila 🐾 N

MYSTERY

Who Stole Mr. T?

Deserae and Dustin Brady

Illustrations by April Brady

Andrews McMeel
PUBLISHING®

Other Books by Dustin Brady

CONTENTS

SNOW DAY

"Nugget, I think . . ."

POOMF!

". . . we should try . . ."

POOMF!

". . . staying on the . . ."

POOMF!

Leila couldn't finish a single sentence before her pup dove into another snow pile.

"Nugget acts like he's never seen snow before!" Leila's friend Kait said.

"He does this every time it snows," Leila replied. "It's his favorite thing."

Nugget pulled his head out of yet another snow pile and wagged his tail. His face was one big snowball.

"He's the Abominable Snow Dog!" Kait giggled.

"Come on, Mr. Abominable," Leila said. "We'll never get anywhere if you keep this up."

Nugget tilted his head, thought about that for a second, and—*POOMF!*—dove again.

"Nugget likes snow days even more than we do, and he doesn't even go to school," Kait said.

Leila wasn't too sure about that. She hadn't been able to think about anything except for the snow day ever since she'd first heard about the possibility of a storm earlier that week. Leila never paid attention to the news when her parents watched, but when the weather guy said "snow," her head popped up from her mystery book like Nugget's would when he heard the word "treat."

"Did he say 'snow'?" Leila asked.

"Eight to twelve inches in some parts of the viewing area," TV weather guy said.

"Eight to twelve inches?!" Leila squealed.

"Don't count your chickens before they hatch," Leila's mom warned.

Oh, the chickens would be counted. That week, the only thing that Leila and all the other students in Mrs. Pierce's third-grade class could talk about was their snow day plans. A lot of kids were going to the Memphis Road sledding hill. A few wanted to make money by shoveling driveways. The Heather Lane crew—Leila, Kait, and their friend Javy—were going to

have a snowball fight and build a snow
fort and make homemade snow cones
and pull each other around on sleds
and then maybe build a snowman or
at least a snow dog. It was going to be
quite a day.

The night before the big day, Leila
stuck a ruler into the ground to
measure snowfall. Five inches or more
and school would be canceled for sure.

She woke up the next morning to something small and furry rolling all over her bed.

"Nugget!" Leila's dad hissed. "Get down! Sorry, honey, I just took him out, and . . ."

Leila didn't hear the rest because she'd just felt the dog with her hand. He was wet. And cold.

"How many inches?!" she asked.

"It's 6:15 a.m.," Leila's dad said. "Why don't you go back to . . ."

"HOW MANY INCHES?!"

Leila's dad smiled. "Eight inches. You got your snow day."

Leila picked up Nugget and danced around her room. "Snow day! Snow day!

Snow day!" Nugget licked her face, then ran to the heat vent to get warm. Leila couldn't fall back asleep because today was a snow day and snow days are the best days.

Finally, she started a video call with the rest of the Heather Lane crew. Javy didn't answer, but Kait did.

"AHHH!" the girls screamed together. They ran through the list of plans for the day, then decided to walk to Javy's and tear their friend out of bed themselves if necessary.

Leila and Kait had gotten about ten steps into their walk before Nugget started his snow-diving routine. Leila sighed while she waited for Nugget to pull his head out of the latest snowdrift.

"I just don't know why . . ."

POOMF!

". . . Javy would still be sleeping . . ."

POOMF!

". . . when we have so much to do."

POOMF!

Kait stopped and stared at a piece of paper freshly taped to a telephone pole. "Oh no," she said.

"What is it?" Leila asked as she leaned in to read the sign. "Oh noooooo."

"MISSING," the sign said over a picture of a turtle.

MISSING

NAME: MR.T

REWARD

ALL MY MONEY ($15.75)
CALL: 216·555·1019
ASK FOR JAVY MARTINEZ

2

TURTLENAPPED

When Leila, Kait, and Nugget reached Javy's house, they found him outside.

"Javy!" Kait yelled when she saw him. "What happened to Mr. T?!"

Javy slumped his shoulders and looked down. Nugget eyed the leftover fliers in his hand.

"I don't know," Javy said. "I haven't seen him since I woke up."

Nugget jumped and grabbed one of the fliers. He started wagging his tail, waiting for Javy to chase him. Javy just looked sad.

"Don't worry! We'll help you find him!" Kait said. "Right, Leila?"

"Oh, uh, yeah, of course!" Leila said. She felt terrible for Javy and really wanted to help him find Mr. T, but she couldn't help but wonder how much this search might cut into their snowball fight.

"Really?" Javy asked. "That's great! Follow me." Javy opened the door and—*CRASH!*—knocked over a pile of boards inside the kitchen. "Oops! I'm so sorry!"

A construction worker with a big, wooly beard shook his head and helped Javy pick up the boards.

"My parents are getting the kitchen remodeled today," Javy explained to Leila and Kait as he finished stacking. "No snow days for construction guys."

Javy led the girls to a side room attached to the kitchen. "Mr. T was right here in his winter home," he said.

Javy's family had turned their pantry into a turtle paradise. The walls were covered with pictures of Javy's family posing with Mr. T and drawings of the turtle dressed in funny costumes. A wooden box piled high with dirt and moss took up every inch of floor space. The box held a small pool, a heat lamp, and a few rocks and logs but no turtle.

"I have some ideas about what might have happened," Javy said. Then, he glanced at the two workers in the kitchen and lowered his voice. "Come to my room."

The kids walked down the hall to Javy's room. When they reached the carpet, Nugget pushed himself all over the floor to dry himself off. Kait started to take off her coat before thinking better of it. "It's cold in here," she said.

Javy nodded. "My dad likes to see how late in the year he can go without turning the heat on," he said. "He must be trying to beat his record."

"When was the last time you saw Mr. T?" Leila asked, eager to find this turtle so they could get back on schedule with the snow day plans.

Javy plopped onto his bed. "Last night before bed. When I woke up this morning—poof! He was gone! I looked all over the house, but he's nowhere."

"Have your parents seen him?" Leila asked.

Javy shook his head. "My mom's working from home today, so she helped me look for a while. I called my dad at work, but he hasn't seen him either."

"What do you think happened?" Kait asked.

"I think he escaped," Javy said. "Sometimes we let him out so he can walk around the house. But when you do that, you've got to keep an eye on him. The construction guys have been going in and out of the house ever since they got here early this morning. I think they left the door open and Mr. T ran away." Javy buried his head between his knees.

Kait moved closer and tried to make Javy feel better. "I mean, Mr. T is a turtle," she said with a smile. "He probably didn't run anywhere."

Javy sniffed a few times. "You know what I mean. I just don't know why he would want to leave in the first place. He hates the cold!"

Leila sat up. Javy had just reminded her of the book she'd been reading earlier that morning—*The Ice Cold Case*. It was a mystery that took place at a frozen pond (she'd picked it out in honor of the snow day). The detective in the book figured out that the thief was a raccoon by following prints in the snow. "If Mr. T went outside, we should be able to follow his tracks in the fresh snow, right?" Leila asked.

Javy perked up. "That's a great idea!"

Leila led the way to the side door. She was feeling great about her plan until she looked down. The snow by the door was almost packed solid with prints from the kids, the workers, Javy's parents, and Nugget. There was no way they could find turtle tracks in this mess. "Let's follow some of these away from the house where the snow isn't so packed," Leila suggested.

The biggest clump of tracks went down the driveway, so the kids followed those first. Unfortunately, they all ended at the bright red construction van parked at the end of the driveway. Next, they got excited when Kait spotted paw prints cutting across the front yard, but then Leila reminded everyone that's where they'd just walked with Nugget. Finally, they followed a set of prints that Javy guessed belonged to his dad going to the garage, but they didn't find any turtle tracks that way either.

"He must have gotten out before it started snowing," Javy said. "That was a good idea, though, Leila."

Kait grabbed Leila's arm. "Look!" She pointed to a single set of suspicious footprints that walked

through Javy's backyard, to the back patio, then turned back to the neighbor's yard.

"Javy," Kait said. "What if Mr. T didn't run away at all?"

"What do you mean?" Javy asked.

Kait's eyes were wide. "What if he got turtlenapped?!"

THE WICKED WITCH OF WEST 73RD STREET

Kait gasped. "If Mr. T got turtlenapped, then this is a real-life mystery!"

Javy looked down. "I don't care about a mystery. I just want my friend back."

"You don't understand," Kait said. "This is great news! You're standing next to the best detective in town."

Javy looked up, surprised. "Leila?" he asked.

Leila gave Kait a weird look. "What are you talking about?"

Kait ignored her. "Leila's read basically every mystery book, so she knows all the tricks. Just the other day, she helped me solve the mystery of my missing Halloween candy."

"I reminded you that you ate it all," Leila said.

"See—isn't she good? She'll catch the turtlenapper before lunchtime!"

"Could you?" Javy asked hopefully.

Leila knew she was no detective, but she did very much want to find Mr. T in time to at least build a snow fort. "We'll do our best," Leila said.

Kait squealed. "What should we do first?!"

Leila looked at the suspicious footprints. "We should probably follow these, right?"

"See?" Kait said to Javy. "Just like a real detective!"

The gang followed the footprints from Javy's back door to a row of bushes along the back of the yard. Javy stopped at the bushes when he saw whose house the tracks had come from.

"Mrs. Crenshaw." He shook his head. "I should have known."

"She doesn't like Mr. T?" Leila asked.

Javy pointed to the snow-covered bushes. "These are Mrs. Crenshaw's rose bushes," he said. Then he pointed to a short wire fence next to the bushes. "And that's Mr. T's summer home. Every year, Mr. T manages to eat half of Mrs. Crenshaw's roses through his pen, and every year she gets sooo mad."

Leila scrunched up her face. "Mad enough to break into your house and steal your pet six months later?" she asked. "That's pretty mean."

"Oh, she's mean all right," Kait said. "So mean! Remember that business I started last year? The one where I sold cool fall leaves?"

Leila remembered Kait's grandma giving her a quarter for some leaves Kait had found, which is not exactly a business, but she didn't argue. "I remember."

"Well, Mrs. Crenshaw yelled at me for picking leaves off her tree! Can you believe it?"

"It is her tree," Leila pointed out.

"It was the FALL!" Kait exclaimed. "They were going to FALL off in a couple days anyways. She's like a witch, she's so mean!"

"That's not kind to say about someone," Leila said. "It just sounds like she wants to keep her trees nice."

"So she can use them for witch things," Kait mumbled.

"I wouldn't say she's a witch," Javy said, "but she's lived behind us ever since I was little, and I don't think she's come over even once. Don't you think it's suspicious that she shows up the very morning that Mr. T goes missing?"

Leila had to admit that it did seem odd.

"How are we going to catch her?" Kait asked. Then her eyes lit up. "Do we get to spy?!"

Leila knew how much Kait loved spying on people, but she had a better idea. "How about we just ask her?" she suggested.

Kait made a face. "I'm not going over there."

"Why not? It'll be fun!"

"Fun? That doesn't sound . . ."

PIFF!

Leila interrupted Kait by hitting her with a snowball square in the chest. "Come on," Leila said. "We'll have fun in the snow and solve a mystery at the same time."

Kait cracked a smile, then tackled Leila. Nugget piled on top.

Javy didn't join in the fun. "Sorry for ruining the snow day, guys. Why don't you two have a snowball fight and I'll talk to Mrs. Crenshaw myself?"

Leila felt bad for slowing Javy's search. She stood up and brushed the snow off her clothes. "No, we'll help you. Right, Kait?"

Kait dropped the big, juicy snowball she'd been building. "Right. Of course."

Since Mrs. Crenshaw lived behind Javy and the kids felt she might get mad at them if they tromped through her backyard, they walked around the block to get to the front door.

"What do we say when we get there?" Javy asked.

"YOU'RE UNDER ARREST!" Kait yelled. "Then we handcuff her."

"Let's just ask her if she knows what happened to Mr. T," Leila said.

"If she did take him, won't she just lie?" Javy asked as they rounded the corner onto W. 73rd Street.

"If she tries to lie, she'll mess up, and we'll catch her. That's what always happens in the books," Leila said, even though she had no idea how to catch someone in a lie.

"If she answers the door riding on a broom, I'm running back home before she can get me," Kait said.

Leila rolled her eyes as she turned up Mrs. Crenshaw's driveway. "Be nice." She scooped up Nugget right before they got to the door. She'd learned a long time ago that a small, waggly tailed dog can make even the meanest adults nice.

Leila took a deep breath to gather her courage. The house was old and a little creepy. She stood in front of the door for a second and knocked. The door opened after just one knock, and a tall woman with straight gray hair answered.

"What do you want?" the woman asked.

Lo and behold, she was holding a broom.

"AH!" Kait ran off the porch.

PRIVATE EYE

"We're, um, looking for his turtle," Leila stammered. "Can you help us?"

Mrs. Crenshaw looked at Leila and Javy, and then at Nugget, who even someone like Mrs. Crenshaw would have to admit looked cute with his tongue sticking out. "Come in," she said.

"Oh, no," Javy said. "It's OK. We were just . . ."

"Come in so I can close this door and stop letting all the heat out!" Mrs. Crenshaw snapped. Javy and Leila quickly stepped inside.

"The dog stays on the mat," Mrs. Crenshaw instructed. Leila set Nugget down and told him to sit. Nugget sat still except for his wagging tail.

"You two came at a good time. Can you hold this for me?" Mrs. Crenshaw handed Javy a dustpan.

"Oh, uh, sure," Javy said. While Javy helped Mrs. Crenshaw sweep the floor, Leila looked around. The house was brighter than she'd expected. Everything seemed to sparkle— especially the kitchen.

While everyone else was distracted, Nugget crept toward a tote bag next to the door. Maybe there were treats inside.

"No!" Mrs. Crenshaw yelled.

Too late. Nugget had already shoved his head and half his body inside, so when he looked at her, he was half dog, half bag.

"I'm so sorry!" Leila reached for Nugget. Before she could catch him, Nugget heard the heater turn on, shook off the bag, and curled up in front of the vent.

Mrs. Crenshaw seemed to be losing patience. "The dog needs to go."

"Wait!" Javy said. "We're looking for my pet turtle. Have you seen him?"

"Not since he finished off the last of my roses this summer," Mrs. Crenshaw answered flatly.

Javy's face turned red. "OK," he said as he turned to leave. "Thank you for your time."

Leila wasn't about to give up that easily. "This morning," she said. "Did you see him when you went to Javy's house this morning?"

That seemed to startle Mrs. Crenshaw. Perfect. Good detectives are always startling people. "How did you know that?" Mrs. Crenshaw asked. "Were you spying on me?"

"Oh, no!" Leila said. "I was just, uh, I mean . . ."

Javy jumped in. "Leila's a detective!"

That made Mrs. Crenshaw crack a small smile for the first time all morning. "A detective?"

Leila blushed. "Oh, no, not really a detective. I mean, well, you see, we noticed footprints going from your house to Javy's back door. And so we were wondering what you were doing there this morning. That's all."

Mrs. Crenshaw tilted her head a bit, a full smile on her face now. "You followed footprints? That sure sounds like something a detective would do."

Leila blushed even redder.

"Well," Mrs. Crenshaw said, "this morning, I recognized the red van in the Martinezes' driveway. It was the same company that helped me with my bathroom. Did you notice the name on the van?"

Leila shook her head.

"You need to pay attention to these things," Mrs. Crenshaw said. "That's what good detectives do. It's 'Margolis

Construction.' Anyway, they did a fine job on my bathroom, but they never took their shoes off and tracked mud everywhere. It took me a week to scrub everything. I warned Mrs. Martinez so she wouldn't have the same problem."

"So you didn't take Mr. T?" Javy asked.

"No, dear," Mrs. Crenshaw said. "That turtle and I are not friends, but I would never do anything like that."

"I know," Javy sighed. "I just really wanted to find him, and I thought maybe . . . I don't know . . ."

"It's OK," Mrs. Crenshaw said. "You've got to follow the clues.

And I did actually see your turtle
this morning."

"Really?!" Javy perked up.

Mrs. Crenshaw nodded. "While I was
talking to your mom, I noticed your dad
holding the turtle in the hallway."

"Oh, wow!" Javy said. "Do you
remember what time it was?"

"Around 7:15."

"Thank you!" Leila said. "That's
so helpful!"

"Aren't you going to write that
down?" Mrs. Crenshaw asked.

"What do you mean?"

"It's a clue. You should write it down."

"Oh. Well, I don't really have
anything for a note."

"Let me get you something." Mrs. Crenshaw walked upstairs, then returned a few minutes later with an old hardbound notepad that read "PRIVATE EYE" on the front. She flipped the crinkly pages until she found a blank one. "Why don't you use this?"

Leila wrote down a few clues from their conversation, then flipped

through the book. It was filled with neat handwriting, a few drawings, and lots of green check marks. "What is this?"

"When I was your age, I set up a detective agency in my neighborhood. I'd solve cases for a nickel each. This was my detective notebook. I always knew how much money I'd made because each case I solved got a green check mark."

Leila flipped through the book again, counting all the check marks. "Wow! You were good!"

Mrs. Crenshaw allowed herself another smile. "To be honest, most of my solutions came from books I was reading. Have you ever read Nancy Drew?"

"Of course!" Leila said. "All the ones at the library, at least."

"I read them all at least five times each," Mrs. Crenshaw said. Then she leaned in and raised an eyebrow. "I still have them if you ever want to borrow one."

"Wow!"

Mrs. Crenshaw turned back to Javy. "I'm sorry about your turtle. I know mysteries are no fun when you're the one who's lost a friend."

"I think we'll find him," Javy said. "I trust Leila."

Mrs. Crenshaw nodded. "I know you'll find him. And when you do, we're going to teach him some rosebush manners!"

5

SMUDGE

PIFF!

A snowball hit Leila square
in the face when she left Mrs.
Crenshaw's house.

"Kait!" Leila yelled.

"Did she try to cook you?" Kait asked
when she rejoined her friends.

"What?"

"The witch. Did she try to cook you?"

"You can't keep calling people names," Leila said. "Her name is Mrs. Crenshaw. And, in fact, she gave us an important clue. She saw Mr. T with Javy's dad at—let's see—7:15 this morning."

"That's right before he usually leaves for work," Javy said.

"So your dad probably took the turtle to the vet or something on his way to work," Kait said.

Javy shook his head. "No way. I called him as soon as I woke up, and he didn't know where Mr. T was."

Kait looked at Javy out of the corner of her eye like she felt sorry

for him, then said, "Well, maybe . . .
Never mind."

"What is it?" Javy asked.

"What if he wasn't telling the truth?"

"Are you saying my dad would
lie to me?"

"You're right . . . you're right. I'm
sure he didn't. Your dad seems great."

Leila shot a mean look at Kait. "Why
would you say something like that?"

"It's just . . . OK, one time my cousin
Clara told me a story. You know my
cousin Clara?"

Leila nodded. Cousin Clara was the
one with all the hard-to-believe stories.

"OK, well, one time Clara told me
about her friend Olivia with a bunny

named Smudge. She named him
Smudge because he had a black smudge
between his eyes that looked like
someone had tried to erase something
from his forehead. Anyway, Smudge
was a great bunny, except he pooped
everywhere. Like EVERYWHERE. And
you know that bunny poops look kind of
like chocolate candies, and Olivia had a
two-year-old brother, and . . ."

"I don't understand what this gross
poo story has to do with Mr. T," Javy
interrupted.

"I'm getting there," Kait said. "So one day, Smudge disappears. Olivia looks everywhere, but she never finds him. She figures he's run away. Then, a couple weeks later, she goes to Lake Farm Park—that's the field trip you go on in second grade where they let you milk the cow."

"We know," Leila said. Like Javy, she was also getting impatient with this story.

"Well, sitting right next to the goats is a bunny rabbit that had a black smudge between his eyes. It's Olivia's bunny. She finds out that her parents had gotten mad at the bunny and decided to give it to the farm without telling her."

Javy looked horrified. Leila shook her head. "You're telling us that her parents gave the bunny away because it pooped a lot? Couldn't they have just kept it in the cage more?"

Kait shrugged. "I mean, it was pooping or chewing stuff or something. I forget exactly, but the point is that the bunny was being bad, so her parents gave it away without telling her."

"My dad would never give away Mr. T!" Javy yelled. "He's part of the family!"

Kait shrugged. "So was Smudge."

"You're not helping," Leila hissed. Then she turned to Javy and tried to calm him down. "That story probably wasn't true. Kait's cousin makes stuff up all the time. Let's focus on what we know. We know Mr. T was in the house at 7:15, right?"

Javy took a breath and nodded.

"And we know that there aren't any turtle tracks leaving the house, right?"

Javy nodded again.

"So he's probably still in the house!"

"Unless . . ."

That was all Kait could say before Leila interrupted her. "Why don't we all go back to the house and look for Mr. T again?"

While the kids walked back to the house, they decided that Javy would search the bedrooms, Kait would tackle the bathrooms and office, and Leila would take the living room and kitchen.

"What about Nugget?" Javy asked. "Don't detectives use dogs to find missing people sometimes? Maybe Nugget can sniff out Mr. T?"

Leila glanced at Nugget, who was jumping at falling snowflakes. "I don't think Nugget is that type of dog."

Javy wouldn't give up on his Nugget idea. When they got back to the house, he ran to Mr. T's home. "This is what the detectives do," Javy explained.

"They have the dog sniff something from the missing person so they know what they smell like." Then he paused. "Huh," he said.

"What is it?" Leila asked.

"I was going to have Nugget sniff Mr. T's cave, but it's gone."

"What does it look like?" Leila asked.

"It's an old flower pot."

"Why don't we just split up and start looking?" Leila suggested.

The group went their separate ways. Leila started in the living room with Nugget. Nugget did a great job of searching the room, mostly because he was looking for snacks the whole time. He shoved his nose between cushions, squeezed behind the TV cabinet, and army crawled underneath the chair. No Mr. T, but they did find fifty-seven cents in loose change, some Goldfish snacks, and a checker.

The kitchen was a little tougher because of all the construction, but Leila asked one of the workers for help. The guy with the beard seemed mean, so she asked one with a neck tattoo. He turned out to be nice. He moved boxes and opened cabinets for her, but they still couldn't find Mr. T. Fifteen minutes later, the kids met back in the living room. "Nothing," Leila said.

Javy was now wearing a too-big winter hat that covered half his head, making him look especially mopey. "Are you guys cold too?"

Kait shook her head.

Leila wasn't ready to give up yet. "How about the basement?"

"Mr. T doesn't walk down stairs," Javy said, but he opened the door to the basement anyway. There wasn't much to Javy's basement. A washing machine and dryer stood against one wall, and tool shelves lined another. About the only other thing in the basement was a ping-pong table covered in boxes. Leila walked around once, then started back up the stairs. Javy stopped her.

"Wait," he said. He ran to the ping-pong table and pulled something out of a box. It was a flower pot. He then turned the box upside down, and out fell all of Mr. T's possessions—food, toys, bowl, everything. It was exactly the type of box someone would pack before giving away a turtle.

"No . . ." Javy's voice trailed off. Tears formed in his eyes.

"I'm sure there's a good explanation," Leila said, even though she couldn't possibly imagine what it might be.

Just then, a door closed upstairs.

"Javy," a voice said. "Have you found Mr. T yet?"

Mr. Martinez had come home.

6

THE A-TEAM

Javy ran up the stairs with tears in his eyes. "DAD!" he yelled. "HOW COULD YOU?!"

"This is the number one rule of spying," Kait said to Leila as she followed Javy. "Everyone's a suspect."

"Save it," Leila mumbled.

Upstairs, Mr. Martinez wrapped Javy in his arms. Nugget had also squeezed himself between the father and son, trying to get a free hug.

"What's wrong?" Mr. Martinez asked.

"He was a good turtle!" Javy said between sobs. "He was such a good turtle! How could you give him away?"

"I didn't give him away!" Mr. Martinez looked at Javy, then at Leila and Kait. "Why would you even think that?"

"We followed the clues!" Kait said proudly.

"Clues? What clues?"

Javy laid out all the clues for his father the best he could between tears. "There aren't any turtle tracks outside (*sob*), and Mrs. Crenshaw saw you holding Mr. T this morning (*sob*), and then you packed all his stuff in a box to give away (*sob*)."

"I would never give Mr. T away," Mr. Martinez said. "You know that."

"But the box . . ."

"I packed his stuff to keep it safe during the construction," Mr. Martinez said.

"But you're the only one who left the house," Kait said. "And Mr. T isn't here, so you had to have taken him somewhere."

Mr. Martinez rubbed his forehead. "Javy, the roads are terrible right now, but I came home during my lunch anyway because this is important to me too. I'm here to find Mr. T."

Javy looked unsure, so Mr. Martinez continued. "Have I ever told you how Mr. T got in this family?"

Javy shrugged. "You got him a long time ago, right?"

"Not just a long time ago. I got him when I was exactly your age."

Leila gasped. "But that means that Mr. T must be . . ." she trailed off.

"Old?" Mr. Martinez offered.

Leila blushed.

"Mr. T is actually thirty-two," Mr. Martinez said. "That's a pretty old pet, huh?"

Leila nodded.

"In third grade, I had a teacher named Ms. Stanley. Ms. Stanley was my favorite teacher ever, mostly because she kept a family of turtles right there in the classroom. She nicknamed the turtles the A-Team after the TV show."

Everyone stared blankly at Mr. Martinez.

"The A-Team? You guys know the A-Team, right? They'd make

like flamethrowers and . . . You know what? It's not important. The important thing is that Ms. Stanley had a rule where if you got an A on your homework, you got to help feed the A-Team that day. I wasn't always the best student, but I loved those turtles so much that I worked extra hard and crushed my homework that year. One turtle in particular was my favorite."

"Mr. T?" Javy asked.

Mr. Martinez nodded. "We started doing this thing where I would hold the food up in the air and he would jump for it. He wouldn't do it for anyone else—just me."

"His jump trick?" Javy asked. "I thought all turtles did that."

"It's very rare," Mr. Martinez said. "Anyway, I started coming in early and staying late just to hang out with Mr. T. Ms. Stanley must have noticed how much I'd bonded with the turtle because she took me aside one day and asked if I'd like to keep him." Mr. Martinez smiled at the memory.

"I was so excited that I dragged my mom to the store that night so we could buy every turtle toy they had. I don't think I slept for three nights. Well, the day finally arrived when I was supposed to take Mr. T home. It was the last day of school before

Christmas break. I showed up to school with a box that had Mr. T's name on it. Only he was gone."

Kait gasped.

"That's how I felt too," Mr. Martinez said. "Ms. Stanley said that she'd taken him out of his home that morning to clean everything for me, and that's when he'd disappeared. She had the whole class search for Mr. T, but nobody found him. After a few hours, everybody else had forgotten about him. We had a party and watched a movie. Want to guess which movie it was?"

The kids kept their mouths shut, partly because they wanted the story to keep going but also because they couldn't think of any movies that old.

"It was the A-Team holiday special," Mr. Martinez said. "That made me feel even worse. I remember that the heat was broken that day, so we all wore our coats in the classroom. I buried my head in my coat like a turtle and cried through the whole movie."

Leila thought about how she'd feel if she ever lost Nugget. She decided that it must be the worst feeling in the world. "What happened?" she asked.

"When class was over, I walked out behind a kid named Manny. Manny was part of the AV Club, which meant

he helped the teacher wheel in the TV
and hook up the video. I remember
walking slowly as Manny pushed the
TV cart and noticing that his video
equipment backpack had a strange
bulge. I looked closer. The bulge
started squirming."

"Eeps!" Kait shrieked. She was very into this story.

"Manny's desk was next to mine because our last names were so close. I remembered how jealous he'd been that I was getting Mr. T instead of him. I got Ms. Stanley, and we opened the backpack. Sure enough, there was Mr. T."

"Did you have that kid arrested?!" Kait asked.

"He wouldn't even admit to taking the turtle, but I didn't care. I couldn't get mad at him. That's how happy I was to have my buddy back."

Then Mr. Martinez looked at his son. "Javy, I know how it feels to lose a best friend. Believe me, I'd never do that to you."

Javy hugged his dad. "I know, Dad." During the hug, Leila wrote down a few more clues in her detective notebook.

- A-Team
- Ms. Stanley
- Manny

She paused and looked up. "Mr. Martinez, what was Manny's last name?"

"Margolis," he said.

Leila froze and stared at the first clue she'd written at the top of the page. She couldn't believe it. She may have just solved the case.

SPIES

"You OK?" Kait whispered to Leila. "You look like you're gonna hurl."

"We need to talk to Javy," Leila whispered. "Alone."

"Hey, Javy," Kait stuck her face between Javy and his dad. "You drew up plans for a snow fort, right? Wanna show them to us?"

"What plans?" Javy asked. "I told you I'm not building a snow fort. We need to . . ."

Kait grabbed Javy's arm and started dragging him away. "They're in your room, right? Let's go!"

Javy tried to push off, but Kait had a vice grip. "Don't wait for us, Mr. Martinez!" she said. "Why don't you eat your lunch and get back to work? Yum, yum!"

"Yum, yum?" Leila asked when Javy's door closed behind them.

"Snow fort?!" Javy yelled. "I told you two—if you want to play in the snow, that's fine. But this is important to me! So you can . . ."

"Hush," Kait interrupted. "Leila solved the case."

Javy's eyes got wide.

"And just so you know, this is important to us too," Leila said. "I was really looking forward to the snow day, but you're my friend, and now I want to help you get Mr. T back more than anything."

"Thank you," Javy said. "Now what did you find?"

Everyone's eyes were on Leila. Even Nugget had jumped onto the bed and was staring at her. She suddenly got a chill. "I, well . . . actually, I'm pretty cold."

Kait threw Leila a blanket. "Just spit it out!" she said.

Leila wrapped up and settled down. "It's the first clue I wrote down," she said. "Look." She showed Javy and Kait the name on the red van outside of Javy's house—Margolis Construction.

"Okayyyyy," Javy said.

"Manny's last name was Margolis," Leila explained.

Kait gasped. "The turtlenapper is back to finish the job!"

"But why would my dad hire Mr. Margolis if he knows he's a turtlenapper?" Javy asked.

"That's what I've been trying to figure out," Leila said. "Maybe it's a different Margolis."

Javy shook his head. "I don't think so. I heard my dad speaking Spanish with another man early this morning. I couldn't hear everything they were saying, but it sounded like they'd grown up together."

"Javy, I don't know why your dad trusts Mr. Margolis, but I think we're going to have to be the ones to catch him," Leila said.

"How?" Javy asked. "Do we question him?"

"NO!" Kait shouted. "WE SPY!"

Leila sighed. "I hate to say it, but Kait might be right. I think we need to spy."

Kait pumped her fist. "First, we need a distraction."

Bark! Bark!

Everyone turned to Nugget. He stood on the edge of the bed, wagging his tail. Kait smiled. "Welcome to the team."

WEIRDY BEARDY

The kids waited until Javy's dad was ready to go back to work.

"Javy, I'm leaving!" Mr. Martinez shouted from the kitchen. "Do I get a hug goodbye?"

Leila, Kait, and Nugget waited in the bedroom while Javy said goodbye to his dad and then secretly scattered chunks of string cheese throughout the kitchen. A minute later, Javy came back to the room and nodded. Leila then whispered Nugget's three favorite words into the dog's ear. "Find the treats!"

Nugget tore out of the room and sprinted through the house until he found the first chunk of cheese in the dining room. He leaped over a pile of tile on the ground and continued his search inside the kitchen.

"I'm so sorry!" Kait said to the startled workers who had to pause while a furry ball of energy bounded around, sniffing everything in sight.

The kids pretended to chase Nugget while actually searching every nook and cranny for signs of turtlenapping.

"Nugget, come back!" Javy yelled while he poked his head into a toolbox.

"You're not being a good dog!" Leila said as she opened a cabinet. She made sure to yell the "good dog" part of the sentence extra loud so Nugget knew he was doing a great job.

Kait flipped a cardboard box upside down, dumping out covers for power outlets and heater vents. "I can use this box to catch him!" she announced. When she found nothing interesting inside, she moved on to another box

and dumped that one too. "Or maybe this would be better!"

The two workers (nicknamed "Weirdy Beardy" and "Tattoo Tom" by Kait) waited patiently while the little show in front of them continued. When the kids finally decided that the turtle was no longer in the kitchen, Leila swooped Nugget up into her arms and apologized to the workers. Time for part two of the plan.

For part two, the kids went outside to build a snow fort. But this wasn't the fort they'd been planning for the last week. No, this would be their special base to sneak into the real target: the van.

Three hours later, the fort was finally complete. Leila curled up with Nugget inside while Javy and Kait crouched nearby. For a few minutes, everything was silent. Leila's heart pounded. This was the most exciting snow day she could have ever imagined!

Weirdy Beardy finally walked out of the house toward the van. Leila took a sharp breath. This was it!

Any second now, Kait would start a snowball fight, then run toward the van. Javy would act like he was throwing a snowball back at Kait, but he'd actually lob it way over her head into the van. Leila would then release Nugget, who'd chase the snowball inside the van. That would give the kids an excuse to enter the van and rescue Mr. T.

It was—they'd all agreed—the perfect plan.

PIFF!

"Ow!" Javy shouted at Kait. "You didn't need to throw it at my face."

"Focus, guys," Leila hissed from her snow fort.

"Can't catch me!" Kait ran toward the van just as Weirdy Beardy opened its back door. Javy made a snowball, wound up, and threw it at the van.

"Go!" Leila turned Nugget loose. The little dog got low to the ground and barreled after the snowball. The snowball was just about to land inside the van, when—

SLAM!

Weirdy Beardy closed the door, and . . .

PIFF!

The snowball exploded when it hit the van door. Nugget stared at the snow spot and then looked back at Leila. Weirdy Beardy left with a long plastic tube under his arm.

Leila jumped out of her snow fort. "Oh no!"

"What do we do now?" Javy asked.

"I . . . I don't know." Leila picked up Nugget. "We could try it again when they come back out, but they'll be expecting it this time. Uh, well, we could . . ."

While Leila's mind was spinning in circles, Kait calmly walked to the van's back door and opened it. "Coming?" she asked.

Leila and Javy stared with their mouths open.

"He didn't lock it. You should have noticed that, detective. Come on."

Leila knew that breaking into the van was wrong, but they were so close! While she argued with herself about what to do, Nugget squirmed out of her arms and jumped into the van. "Nugget, wait!" She followed the dog inside but stopped short when she found Kait and Javy tearing through boxes.

"Guys, come on," Leila said. "We shouldn't be doing this. Mr. T probably isn't even . . ." She stopped midsentence when her eyes landed on a small cooler with a turtle logo on it.

Javy gasped. "Mr. T!"

Before he could tear open the cooler, however, a figure appeared in the doorway.

"What are you doing in my van?!"

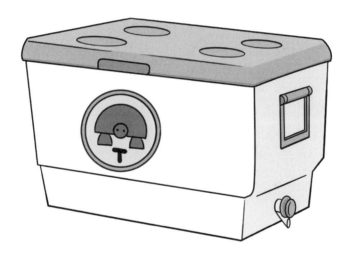

9

TURTLE SOUP

"AHHHHH!" Kait screamed.

"Hey, it's OK," the man said.

"AHHHHH!"

The man's expression changed from anger to concern. "Really, it's OK. I'm not going to hurt you."

"AH! AH! AHHHHHH!" Kait's face turned red.

The man looked around nervously. "Come on, people are going to think I'm kidnapping you or something. Get out of the van and we can talk in the house."

Kait instantly stopped screaming. "OK," she said as she climbed out.

When Leila hopped out of the van, she noticed a Margolis Construction pickup truck parked in the driveway that hadn't been there before. That must be where the man had come from.

Back in the house, the man sat across from the kids at the dining room table. "So now can you tell me why you were snooping in my van?"

Kait stuck her nose up in the air. "Only if you tell us why you're stealing turtles."

"What?!"

Leila decided to jump in. "Are you Manny Margolis?"

"I am."

"You stole my dad's turtle in third grade," Javy shouted. "And you almost got away with stealing him again!"

"OK," Mr. Margolis held up his hand. "I've told your dad a million times—I did NOT steal that turtle in third grade."

Kait rolled her eyes. "Please. We're kids, but we're not stupid. It's pretty hard not to notice a giant turtle in your backpack."

"First of all, that wasn't my backpack," Mr. Margolis said. "That was the AV room backpack, so I didn't know what was inside. Second, Ms.

Stanley was in the room with me the whole time I was setting up, so she would have noticed me stealing a turtle. Third . . ." Mr. Margolis shook his head. "I don't know why I'm explaining all this to you. You're not going to believe me now, just like no one believed me back then. Go ahead. Open the cooler and see for yourself."

Javy opened the cooler, looked inside, then slumped his shoulders. "It's soup," he said.

"Soup?!" Kait screeched. "You turned Mr. T into soup?! YOU MONSTER!"

Weirdy Beardy popped his head into the dining room. "Is that my soup?"

His eyes lit up when he saw the cooler in front of Javy. "Thanks! I was looking all over for this!" He grabbed the cooler and walked out of the dining room.

"I'm super sorry," Leila said.

"It's OK," Mr. Margolis said. "I just wish you would have talked to me rather than look through my stuff. There's some expensive equipment in there. Plus, breaking into someone else's vehicle is a crime, you know."

Leila looked around the room. "Has anyone seen Nugget?"

"Great!" Kait said. "Now we've got two missing animals? Does this house just eat pets?!"

"Here he is." Javy's dad walked into the room holding Nugget. "He was curled up in front of the living room heater." He handed the warm pup to Leila and turned to Javy. "This isn't what I want to see when I come home from work. What's going on?"

"We thought Mr. Margolis had taken Mr. T, but we were wrong," Javy said.

"Why would you think he took Mr. T? Manny's one of my oldest friends!"

"Because he stole Mr. T when you were in third grade! We thought the only reason he'd be here is if he were finishing the job!"

Javy's dad shook his head. "You don't stay mad at someone forever just because they do something one time. You forgive people. Mr. Margolis was my friend all through school. That's why I hired him to do our kitchen!"

Javy looked at the ground. This was their last idea. "We'll never find Mr. T now."

Something about this whole thing had been bothering Leila ever since Javy's dad had handed her Nugget. Finally, she realized what it was— Nugget was toasty warm.

"Mr. Martinez," Leila said. "Has the heat been on all day?"

Javy's dad looked puzzled. "It's been on since last week. Why do you ask?"

Leila smiled. "I think I just solved two cases."

THUNK

Leila ran from room to room, feeling the heater vents. When she got to Javy's bedroom, she squealed. Finally, she sprinted down the steps to the basement while everyone else tried to keep up. "Leila, I told you—Mr. T can't walk down stairs!" Javy said.

"I know that," Leila replied. "He's not in the basement."

"What are you talking about?!" Kait asked.

Without answering, Leila grabbed a broom and looked at the ceiling. Javy's basement didn't have any ceiling tiles, which meant Leila had a clear view to the pipes and ducts above. She walked  to where she guessed the kitchen was and started banging ducts with the handle of her broom.

CLANG!

She walked forward a step and banged again.

CLANG!

She took another step and tried one more time.

THUNK.

Leila tried twice more.

THUNK. THUNK.

"Why does it sound like that?" Javy asked.

Leila smiled. "Because there's a turtle in there!"

Javy's eyes got wide. "No way!"

"Let's go up to your bedroom and find out if I'm right!"

Nugget led the way by galloping up the stairs. Mr. Margolis grabbed a screwdriver from the kitchen and quickly unscrewed the heater vent from the bedroom wall. Javy reached inside. "Feel anything?" his dad asked.

"No," Javy said. Then he reached in a little farther. "Wait!" He leaned in as far as he could, smooshing his face against the wall. He gasped.

"Mr. T!" Javy finally scooped out the turtle. Although Mr. T was a little dusty from the vent, he was alive and looking quite pleased with himself.

"I can't believe you're OK!" Javy gave Mr. T a giant hug, or at least as big of a hug as he could give the turtle with Nugget squeezed in between.

"I'm so confused!" Kait said. "Did Mr. Margolis hide the turtle in there so he could take him later?"

"NO!" Leila and Mr. Margolis shouted at the same time.

"It was all Nugget," Leila explained while she petted her dog. "He loves curling up by the heater when he comes in from the cold. He's done it all day—at my house, in Mrs. Crenshaw's house, and in the living room just now. I just remembered that the only place he hasn't done it is Javy's bedroom. That's because no heat has been coming out of the vent. Notice how cold it is in here compared to the rest of the house? Mr. T's been blocking the heat to this room all day!"

"But how did he get in there in the first place?" Javy asked.

"From the kitchen!" Leila was so excited that she was practically bouncing in place. "Your dad had to let Mr. T out of his turtle home this morning to put his stuff away when the construction guys came. Well, it got cold with them opening the door a bazillion times. We know Mr. T hates the cold—that's why he has a heat lamp and flowerpot cave in his home. So he went to the warmest cave he could find. Kait, do you remember what fell out of the first box you dumped in the kitchen this afternoon?"

Kait's eyes got wide. "The covers for the kitchen heater vents!"

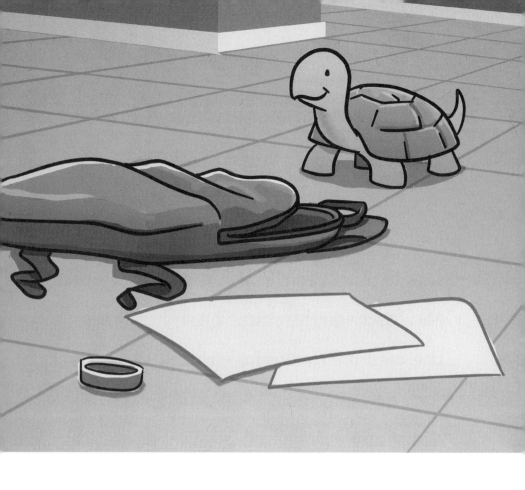

Leila nodded. "So Mr. T crawled
into the duct and tried walking toward
Javy's voice."

"I can't believe he was right here the
whole time!" Javy said.

"You said you solved two mysteries,"
Mr. Margolis said. "Does that mean

you figured out what happened to Mr. T when I was in third grade?"

Leila nodded. "It was cold back then, just like today. Remember? The heat was broken. While the teacher cleaned Mr. T's cage, he must have hidden in the warmest cave he could find."

"The backpack!" Mr. Margolis exclaimed.

Javy's dad turned in shock. "So you really didn't steal Mr. T back then?!"

"That's what I've been telling you for thirty years!" Mr. Margolis said.

The two men did a complicated handshake and hugged. "I should have never doubted you," Javy's dad said.

"And I never should have toilet papered your house to get back at you for doubting me," Mr. Margolis said.

"That was you?!"

"That's THREE mysteries solved!" Kait exclaimed.

"Hey, does anyone know what time it is?" Javy asked.

Kait looked at her watch. "It's 3:30."

"Good."

"Why 'good'?" Kait asked.

"Because that leaves two hours of daylight to get back at you for hitting me in the face with a snowball."

"You've got to catch me first!" Kait squealed as she ran out of the bedroom.

Nugget sprinted after her, excited to finally enjoy the snow day he'd been promised.

11

THE CASE WITH NO CLUES

One week later, Leila was wiping cookie crumbs off her face in Mrs. Crenshaw's kitchen as she wrapped up her story. "Mr. Margolis finished the kitchen remodel a few days later, and he even added extra stuff to Mr. T's room to make it cooler," she said.

"That's wonderful," Mrs. Crenshaw said. "But you never finished your story. Did he ever catch her?"

"Did who catch who?"

"Did Javy ever catch up to Kait and get her back?"

"Oh, yeah," Leila said. "We had the biggest snowball fight ever that afternoon! Toward the end, Javy used Nugget to lure Kait into a trap behind the shed, then he hit her with a snowball so big it could have been a snowman's head!"

Mrs. Crenshaw sat back and chuckled. "Good for him."

"Well, anyway, here's your notebook back." Leila slid the old private eye notebook across the table. "It was great."

"No, no, I want you to keep it," Mrs. Crenshaw said. "You're the new detective on the block now."

"Really?!" Leila asked. "I mean . . . I don't know if I'm really a detective."

"Did you solve a case?" Mrs. Crenshaw asked.

"Well, yeah, but . . ."

"Then you're a detective. End of story. You don't need someone to give you a title for it to be true. Now, did you read any of the other cases in the notebook?"

"Oh! What? Uhhhh, I mean . . ." Leila wasn't normally a snooper like Kait, but if someone hands you a notebook full of real-life mysteries, what are you supposed to do?

"It's OK," Mrs. Crenshaw said. "You probably noticed that all of the cases had green check marks next to them except for one."

Leila had noticed. She flipped back to it. "The Case with No Clues." While most of the other cases had just a handful of notes written underneath the title, this one had four whole pages of questions, maps, arrows, and lots of scribbles.

Mrs. Crenshaw tapped the notebook. "Think you want to give this one a try?"

Leila stared at the title for a second, then looked up, confused. "There aren't any clues?"

"No clues," Mrs. Crenshaw said with a twinkle in her eye. "But there is a treasure."

About the Authors

Deserae and Dustin Brady are the parents of Leila Brady (a girl) and Nugget Brady (a dog). They live in Cleveland, Ohio. Dustin wants to buy a turtle. Deserae does not. If you live with a cute dog, Deserae and Dustin would love to see it! You can email your picture to dustin@dustinbradybooks.com.

April Brady grew up in Maine and has been bringing her imagination to life in pencil since she was a wee lass. Teaming up with her family to tell stories is her favorite thing to do. When she isn't drawing, she gets to have new adventures with her own little girls (the real Leila's cousins). If you like drawing your adventures or pets and family too, she'd be happy to see your art at aprilbradyart@yahoo.com.

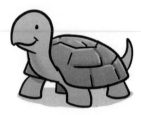

Andrews McMeel Publishing
a division of Andrews McMeel Universal
1130 Walnut Street, Kansas City, Missouri 64106

www.andrewsmcmeel.com

22 23 24 25 26 SDB 10 9 8 7 6 5 4 3 2 1

ISBN Paperback: 978-1-5248-7706-4
ISBN Hardback: 978-1-5248-7825-2

Library of Congress Control Number: 2022935969

Made by:
King Yip (Dongguan) Printing & Packaging Factory Ltd.
Address and location of production:
Daning Administrative District, Humen Town
Dongguan Guangdong, China 523930
1st Printing—6/13/22

ATTENTION: SCHOOLS AND BUSINESSES

Andrews McMeel books are available at quantity discounts with bulk purchase for educational, business, or sales promotional use. For information, please e-mail the Andrews McMeel Publishing Special Sales Department: specialsales@amuniversal.com.